Chicken Licken was sitting under a big tree on the farm.

Suddenly, a nut fell on him!

"Help," cried Chicken Licken. "The skies are falling. I must run and tell the King."

As quick as a flash, Chicken Licken ran to tell him.

Along the road, he met Henny Penny.

"The skies are falling, and I'm off to tell the King," said Chicken Licken.

"Can I come?" said Henny Penny in a panic.

"Yes," replied Chicken Licken.

Chicken Licken and Henny Penny ran to get help.

Along the road, they met Ducky Lucky.

"The skies are falling, and we are off to tell the King," said Chicken Licken.

"Can I come?" begged Ducky Lucky.

"Yes," replied Chicken Licken.

Chicken Licken, Henny Penny, and Ducky Lucky ran to get help.

Along the road, they met Cocky Locky.

“The skies are falling, and we are off to tell the King,” said Chicken Licken.

“Can I come?” said Cocky Locky.

“Yes,” replied Chicken Licken.

Chicken Licken, Henny Penny, Ducky Lucky, and Cocky Locky ran to get help.

Along the road, they met Foxy Loxy.

In a fluster, Chicken Licken said, “The skies are falling, and we are off to tell the King.”

“You are in luck!” said Foxy Loxy, licking his lips. “I am the King. Come in for dinner and tell me all about it.”

But, luckily, Chicken Licken spotted Foxy Loxy's cunning plan.

"Run!" he shouted.

Chicken Licken, Henny Penny, Ducky Lucky, and Cocky Locky ran back to the shelter of the farm.

They all had fresh corn for supper and fell asleep.